THE BIG LEAF PILE

Adapted by Josephine Page
Illustrated by Jim Durk

**Based on the Scholastic book series
"Clifford the Big Red Dog"
by Norman Bridwell**

From the television script
"Leaf of Absence" by Scott Guy

SCHOLASTIC INC.

New York   Toronto   London   Auckland   Sydney   Mexico City
New Delhi   Hong Kong

ISBN 0-439-21357-6

Copyright © 2000 Scholastic Entertainment Inc. All rights reserved.
Based on the CLIFFORD THE BIG RED DOG book series published by Scholastic Inc. TM and © Norman Bridwell.
SCHOLASTIC, CARTWHEEL BOOKS and associated logos are trademarks and/or registered trademarks of Scholastic Inc.
CLIFFORD, CLIFFORD THE BIG RED DOG and associated logos are trademarks and/or registered trademarks of Norman Bridwell.

Library of Congress Cataloging-in-Publication Data available

18 19 20   03 04 05

Printed in the U.S.A.   23
First printing, September 2000

It was a beautiful fall day
on Birdwell Island.
Cleo, Clifford, and T-Bone
were making leaf piles.

Cleo finished her pile
of leaves. They were red, yellow,
orange, gold, and brown.

She counted—

one, two, three—

and jumped in.

Clifford finished his pile
of leaves. They were red, yellow,
orange, gold, and brown.

He counted—

one, two, three—

and jumped in.

T-Bone's pile was not
finished yet. T-Bone's pile
had only brown leaves. Brown
leaves make a nice, loud sound.

"I need more leaves,"

T-Bone said.

"I will help," said Clifford.

"I will help, too," said Cleo.

And they did.

T-Bone's pile of

leaves was ready.

But T-Bone had to go home.

It was time for him

to go for a walk.

"I will watch your leaves,"
said Clifford. "They will
be safe with me. I promise."

"You are a good friend,"

said T-Bone.

And a happy T-Bone trotted off.

Clifford watched the pile
of leaves. He watched
and watched some more.

"This is a very nice leaf pile,"
he said. "I can't wait to hear
its loud sound."
"We could jump in carefully
so we don't mess it up," said Cleo.

"Yes, we could," said Clifford.

"Then let's jump," said Cleo.

The leaves flew.

A strong wind blew them
everywhere.

"Oh, no!" said Clifford.

Clifford and Cleo chased

T-Bone's leaves.

One leaf was

on a weather vane.

Another leaf was

under the mail truck.

Clifford and Cleo found a leaf

on a swing in the playground.

They found a leaf

on some french fries.

Clifford and Cleo found every

one of the missing leaves.

"This is a great leaf pile,"

said Clifford.

"I can't wait to hear

the noise it makes," said Cleo.

"We could jump in,"
Clifford said.

"But we won't,"

they said together.

T-Bone came back.

His pile looked even bigger

and better than before.

"Thank you for watching

my leaves," he said to Clifford.

"I want you to be the first

to jump in."

"We must tell you the truth.
We already jumped into your pile.
All your leaves flew away,"
Clifford said. "But Cleo and I got
them back. I'm sorry, T-Bone."

"I'm glad you told me the truth,"
said T-Bone. "I still want you
to jump in first."

So Clifford jumped in

with a big *CRUNCH!*

Then Cleo and T-Bone jumped in.

CRUNCH! CRUNCH!

And the three friends enjoyed

the rest of the beautiful

fall day.

Do You Remember?

Circle the right answer.

1. The names of the characters in the story are...
   a. Clifford, Nero, and T-Bone.
   b. Clifford, Cleo, and T-Bone.
   c. Clifford, Nero, and T-Shirt.

2. T-Bone's leaves are...
   a. red, yellow, gold, and brown.
   b. all yellow.
   c. all brown.

Which happened first?
Which happened next?
Which happened last?
Write a 1, 2, or 3 in the space after each sentence.

T-Bone had to go home. _____

T-Bone made
a brown leaf pile. _____

Clifford and Cleo found a leaf
under a mail truck. _____

Answers: